JULIET MALEVOLENT...
AN EVIL TALE

Written by Peta-Gaye Nash
Illustrated by Colin McClean

GMJ
Creative Hands Inc.

This is a work of fiction. Any resemblance to anyone, living or dead,
is purely coincidental.

Published in Canada in 2015 by GMJ Creative Hands, Inc.
ISBN 978-0-9813799-3-7

For Isabella and Jolie

This work was produced, in part, through the generous support of Julia Brown, Patron of the Arts.

Even before **Juliet Malevolent** went to **KINDEREVILGARTEN**, her parents suspected she was different. She didn't pull the cat's tail or torment the dog. Instead, she cuddled the cat and walked the dog three times a day.

She didn't pout and sulk at the dinner table and she ate almost everything on her plate without complaining. She even **thanked** her parents for breakfast, lunch and dinner.

Her brother, **MALCOLM MALEVOLENT**, on the other hand, misbehaved perfectly. He refused to eat his dinner and sometimes even threw it on the floor. His parents were quite proud of him.

Every morning in **KINDEREVILGARTEN** the class had to stand and recite their vow:

"I will do my best to be naughty and annoying, troublesome and tiresome, and to be a pest to society whenever possible! This is my evil vow!"

Between learning their letters and writing, they had to perform some evil tasks. **TOMMY TOMFOOLERY** put glue on **MS. TERMAGANT'S** seat so that she was stuck to her chair all day and couldn't get up. **MS. TERMAGANT** said **TOMMY** was very clever!

GISELLE GENERALTROUBLEMAKER

would not sit still for a moment. She ran around the classroom wreaking havoc, throwing the crayons, painting the walls, and hiding the other children's jackets and shoes.

When it was recess time, no one could find their jackets and everyone had to stay inside. "**GISELLE** is a real troublemaker," said **MS. TERMAGANT** in a proud voice.

TANYA TEMPERAMENTAL refused to listen and she sat on the floor and threw a tantrum. She screamed until her face turned red. "Impressive!" said **MS. TERMAGANT**.

Now what about you, **Juliet**? What evil thing will you do for us today?" **Juliet** thought and thought and thought. "I could help you clean the walls," she suggested.

"No!" screamed **MS. TERMAGANT.**

Juliet, please repeat the school vow!" **MS. TERMAGANT** yelled.

Juliet repeated the school vow:

"I will do my best to be naughty and annoying, troublesome and tiresome, and to be a pest to society whenever possible! This is my evil vow!"

Now," said **MS. TERMAGANT** in her most evil voice. "What evil thing will you do today, Juliet? Will you hide the pencils? Will you turn over the paint? Will you refuse to do your homework?"

"**MS. TERMAGANT**, I really don't want to be evil. I've done my homework," replied Juliet.

Juliet, this homework is neat and very well done. I'm afraid I have to give you a **ZERO**!"

Student Name: Juliet Malevolent

Category	Exceeds The Standard	Meets The Standard	In Progress	Does Not Meet
Grade	A	B	C	0

	First Semester	Second Semester	Third Semester
Not Sharing	0		
Rude Behaviour	0		
Introduction To Evil Math	0		
Not Listening	0		
Mad Science	0		
Horrible Art	0		
Introduction To Pranking	0		
Final Mark	0		

Comments:

Juliet gets a zero for __NOT__ being evil. She is kind, caring and compassionate. This will simply __NOT__ do!

That semester, **Juliet's** report card read:

"Juliet gets a zero for <u>NOT</u> being evil. She is kind, caring and compassionate. This will simply <u>NOT</u> do!"

The next school semester was the same thing. **TOMMY TOMFOOLERY** was at the top of the class for putting a frog in **MS. TERMAGANT'S** purse. She screamed in fright when she saw it but she applauded **TOMMY** for a job well done.

"That was so evil, **TOMMY**!" she said in a delighted voice.

Student Name: Juliet Malevolent

Academic Performance Level For Learning				
Category	Exceeds The Standard	Meets The Standard	In Progress	Does Not Meet
Grade	A	B	C	0

	First Semester	Second Semester	Third Semester
Not Sharing	0	0	
Rude Behaviour	0	0	
Introduction To Evil Math	0	0	
Not Listening	0	0	
Mad Science	0	0	
Horrible Art	0	0	
Introduction To Pranking	0	0	
Final Mark	0	0	

Comments:

Juliet has failed again. This time she was even more helpful, thoughtful and even nicer than last semester. We simply do not know what to do with her. She refuses to be evil. She won't even pull a harmless prank.

Juliet, however, got another bad report card. It read:

"Juliet has failed again. This time she was even more helpful, thoughtful and even nicer than last semester. We simply do not know what to do with her. She refuses to be evil. She won't even pull a harmless prank."

I can't help it," said Juliet to her DAD when she showed him her report card. "I don't want to be evil. I want to be good and do nice things for people."

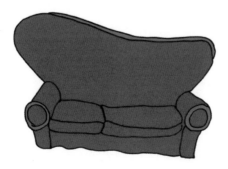

B ut we're evil," said her **DAD**. "We're not supposed to do nice things for people. **MS. TERMAGANT** says you helped GISELLE with her math and you were kind to everybody, even to... **TANYA TEMPERAMENTAL!**"

"I just can't be evil, **DADDY**. I try so hard to be like everybody else but I can't be. I'm not good at being evil. I'm sorry." Tears came to Juliet's eyes.

There, there. Don't cry. We want you to be happy. Perhaps you should just be yourself," he said comforting her. "But why do you want to be good? No one else is good."

"Being good makes me feel great," she said and she threw her arms around her **DAD** and gave him a great big, non-evil hug!

The next day while **Juliet** was walking to school... a wicked wind blew through the schoolyard.

The project that Juliet had been working on all week was lifted out of her arms, carried through the air and smashed against a tree.

TOMMY TOMFOOLERY saw it happen. **Juliet** started to cry. **TOMMY** was about to laugh at her because that would be truly evil.

Then he remembered how **Juliet** had shared her lunch with him the day he had forgotten his lunch at home. He rushed to help her and picked up the pieces of the project.

GISELLE GENERALTROUBLEMAKER saw it too. She was about to laugh but then she remembered how Juliet had helped her with her math homework. She also rushed over to help.

TANYA TEMPERAMENTAL saw it and was about to tattle to MS. TERMAGANT and tell her that Juliet didn't have her homework. Tattling would be really malicious. But then she remembered how Juliet had held her hand when she was having one of her temper tantrums. TANYA immediately went to help Juliet.

Together they gathered the pieces of the project and glued it back together. It looked as good as new.

From that moment on the children realized that doing nice things for each other felt great. And when they went into class that morning, **TOMMY** gave **MS. TERMAGANT** his apple. **TANYA** helped her to clean the paint from the walls. **GISELLE** removed the glue from all the seats. **Juliet** smiled a great big non-evil smile!

I think **MS. TERMAGANT** was grateful for all that niceness. Don't you?

Glossary

Compassionate - kind behaviour; having a desire to help others

Malevolent - wishing evil to others

Malicious - mean; wanting to hurt someone

Tattle - to tell another person's wrongdoing

Temperamental - moody behaviour

Termagant - an overbearing, violent or brawling woman

Tomfoolery - foolish behaviour; nonsense

Peta-Gaye Nash is a Jamaican-born short story writer. Her work has appeared in *Canadian Voices*, Volume 2, Bearing Witness Anthologies and *Bookends*: the Jamaica Observer's Literary Magazine. *I Too Hear the Drums* is her 2010 collection. She recently published five children's books: *Essie Wants an Education, Don't Take Raja to School, Liam and the Lizard, Is Reine Still Sleeping* and *Where Are Meadow's Manners?* A graduate of McMaster University, Peta-Gaye teaches English as a Second Language in Mississauga, ON, Canada where she lives with her family. To learn more about Peta-Gaye and her passion for writing visit **PetagayeNash.com**.

Colin McClean is an author, illustrator and challenge coach. In 2004, he founded LLSCartoons, a marketing communications design firm that specializes in simplifying complex information through design. It was an extension of his weekly comic strip, *Life's Lighter Side...*, which was published from 2001-2010. In 2013, he established **ColinMcClean.com** to expand his passion for helping others to grow. Using the comedic edge that propelled the comic strip and his book illustrations, Colin continues to make people laugh, while helping them to grow their businesses.

Made in the USA
Columbia, SC
30 December 2017